My Home

by Reneé Bartkowski

illustrated by ROFry

GOLDEN PRESS
Western Publishing Company, Inc.
Racine, Wisconsin

Eighth Printing, 1979

If I were a deer, I would make my home
In a forest that's shady and cool;
If I were a frog, I'd live by the side
Of a clear and shimmering pool.

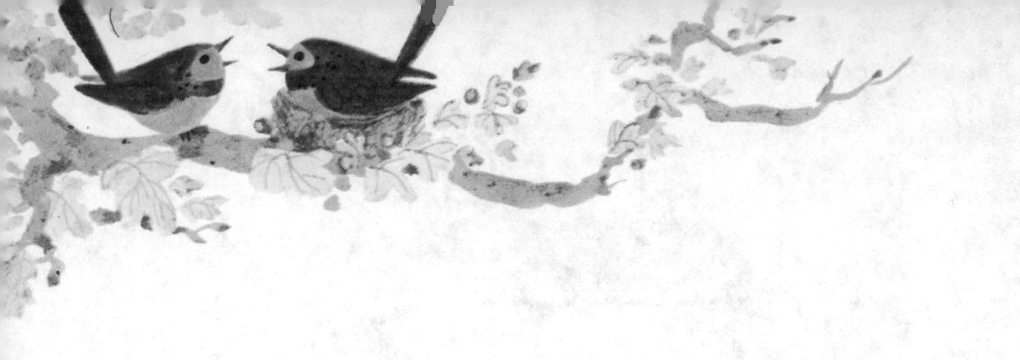

If I were a bird, I would build my nest
High on the branch of a tree,

And a small busy hive would be my home,
If I were a buzzing bee.

If I were a gopher,

I'd

burrow

right

down

In the earth, so snug and deep,

And if I were a bear, I'd find a spot
In a cave for my winter's sleep.

If I were a tiger, I'd make my home
In a jungle thick with trees;

If I were a whale, I'd live and roam
In the depths of the vast blue seas.

If I were a cow, I'd live on a farm
With hens and hogs and sheep,
And a big red barn with sweet-smelling hay
Would shelter me when I sleep.

If I were a horse, I'd live in a stable,
With a pasture near my door,

And if I were a clam, I'd live in the sand
On a white and glistening shore.

But I'm not a clam, or a lamb, or a frog,
Or a bird who lives in a tree.
And I'm not a horse, or a hen, or a hog,
Or a little brown gopher—I'm me!

I can't live in a cave, as some animals can,

Or high on the branch of a tree,

And I can't
burrow
down
in a hole in the ground,

Or live in the depths of the sea.

But I could live in a home on the top of a hill—
In a cottage beside the shore;

I could live in a house with a big front porch
And a garden near my door.

I could live in a trailer that moves all about
The beautiful countryside.

I could live in a houseboat that drifts slowly by
On rivers so deep and wide.

I could live on a farm, in a house that's small,
Near fields of golden wheat,

Or high in a building that stands so tall,
On a bustling city street.

I could live in a cabin of rustic logs,
High on a mountaintop,

Or in bright sunny rooms that stand behind
A quaint little grocery shop.

It doesn't matter at all if my home's big or small,
If it's brown or yellow or white;
It doesn't matter at all if it's narrow or tall,
Or if it is pretty or bright.

It doesn't matter at all if my home's on a hill,
Or down by the deep blue sea—
As long as it's filled with people I love,
And people who also love me.